TIME
FOR
JODY

Harper & Row, Publishers

New York · Evanston · San Francisco · London

TIME
FOR
JODY

by Wendy Kesselman
Pictures by Gerald Dumas

Time for Jody
Text copyright © 1975 by Wendy Kesselman
Pictures copyright © 1975 by Gerald Dumas
All rights reserved. No part of this book may be used or reproduced in any manner whatsoever without written permission except in the case of brief quotations embodied in critical articles and reviews. Printed in the United States of America. For information address Harper & Row, Publishers, Inc., 10 East 53rd Street, New York, N.Y. 10022. Published simultaneously in Canada by Fitzhenry & Whiteside Limited, Toronto.
Library of Congress Catalog Card Number: 75–6295
Trade Standard Book Number: 06–023138–6
Harpercrest Standard Book Number: 06–023139–4
First Edition

For Mark

In a cozy burrow
Jody the groundhog
lived with her mother and father.
Jody loved sleeping.
She fell asleep in the morning
brushing her teeth.
She fell asleep
munching crunchy onions at lunch.
She fell asleep
playing Sleeping Beauty with her friends.

Winter was Jody's favorite time.
For then she curled up in the cozy burrow
and slept until her father woke her for spring.
Jody's father was very important.
It was his job to wake
all the animals in the field
and tell them spring had come.
On February 2, he would poke his head
out of the warm burrow. If the sun was shining
and he saw his shadow on the ground,
he knew that winter was not yet over,
and he would tumble back into bed.

Six weeks later he would come out again.
This time he would run through the field
calling, "Spring's here, everybody!"
And all the animals would come out of their holes.

One fall day there was a thump at the door.
Jody peeked out.
There stood a large rabbit, puffing hard.
"I have a letter here
for someone called Jody," he puffed.
"I've hopped all the way from the Distant Field."
Jody ran to the door.
She had never gotten a letter before.
"I'm Jody," she cried. "Where's my letter?"
"Are you really Jody?" asked the rabbit.
"We were expecting someone bigger. Besides—
you're a girl. We were expecting a boy."
"I'm not so small," said Jody. "And
what's wrong with being a girl?"

Jody snatched the letter from the rabbit's paw.
"My name's Jody," she muttered to herself,
"and that's my letter."
The rabbit laughed.
"That's some little girl you have there,"
he said to Jody's mother and father.
"We think so," they said proudly.
"Listen!" cried Jody. "It's an invitation."

Dear Jody,

We the animals of the Distant Field would like to invite you to come and be our groundhog. For one thing, we don't have one. For another thing, we've heard that your father is a very good groundhog and we're hoping it runs in the family. Usually we never wake up till summer.

Best Wishes and Please Come Soon,
Your friends,
the squirrels, turtles, raccoons,
snails, bears, and rabbits
of the Distant Field.

"When can I go?" Jody asked. "Tomorrow?"
"We'll see," said her father,
which was what he always said.
Her mother smiled.
That night, for the first time,
Jody couldn't fall asleep.
Lying in her warm bed she made up a little song.

I am going
To a place I've found
Where the fields tumble down,
Where the crickets sing to greet me
When I'm sleeping oh so sweetly
And I'm so happy!

I am going
To have new friends there
Rabbits, turtles, raccoons, and bear
Where the onions are so munchy
When I'm crunching, crunching, crunching
And I'm so happy!

Yes, I'm going
I can hardly wait
For the day when I will wake
All the animals who wrote me
I am going where I'll be
Oh so happy!

The song grew softer and softer
and slower and slower.
"I am going," Jody sang,
"Where the crickets sing to greet me
When I'm sleeping oh so sweetly. . . ."
And she was, too.

A few days later
Jody was taking a nap under the old apple tree.
"Wake up, Jody! Wake up!"
A crow flew down and tickled her toes with his beak.
"You better wake up," he said. "Something's
happening at your house."
"What?" Jody yawned, and she stumbled home.

Down in the burrow there wasn't a sound.
"That crow was all wrong," Jody said. "Nothing's
happening here at all."

"SURPRISE! SURPRISE!"
There were her parents and grandparents,
her aunts and uncles,

and seventeen cousins all in a row.

"It's a going-away party," said her grandmother,
"because we're so proud of you."
They were all holding packages.
"For me?" asked Jody. "For you," they said.
Jody unwrapped her mother's present first.
"It's beautiful!" she cried,
taking out a shiny red alarm clock.
"Just what I need to wake up February 2."

Next she unwrapped a small green alarm clock.
"Oh," said Jody. "This one's beautiful, too."
Then there was an enormous grandfather's clock
with a special secret alarm.
"I'll never sleep through this one!"
Jody tore the wrappings off all the presents
and when she had finished, there were
twenty-seven alarm clocks all in a row.
"I guess it always was hard for me to wake up,"
said Jody, laughing. "Anyway, I love them all."

That night Jody wound up all the clocks.
"Tick, tick, tick, tick," they went.
"They sound like crickets," she said. "Hundreds
of crickets. They'll put me to sleep."
"You won't have any trouble waking up
February 2, will you?" asked her mother.
"Oh, no," said Jody. "No trouble at all."

The next day Jody left for the Distant Field.
It had just begun to snow
and there wasn't an animal around.
"Where is everybody?" she asked
the big brown bear who was helping her move.
"Where are the rabbits and the raccoons
and the squirrels and the snails?"

"They're all sleeping," said the bear.
"We go to sleep very early around here."
"I'll just show you to your burrow
and then I'll turn in, too."

Down in her burrow Jody felt lonely,
as lonely as someone can be
who's away from home for the first time.

Jody began a letter to her parents.

Dear Mother and Father,
It's nice here, but very lonely. I miss you.
Maybe you should come and get me.

Then she tore it up.
"That's silly," she said.
"After all, I wanted to come,"
and she started setting all the clocks
for February 2.

"Tick, tick, tick, tick," they went.
"Crickets always did put me to sleep,"
she said, and tumbled into bed.

On February 2, just when they should,
all the clocks went off at once.
Jody yawned. "Oh no, not spring already!"
She poked her head out of the burrow.
"Oh, good. There's my shadow. I can sleep
for six more weeks."
Jody tumbled right back into her soft bed,
so sleepy she forgot to set the clocks
for six weeks ahead.
Down, down, down, she sank
into a warm, wonderful sleep.
"Tick, tick, tick," sang the clocks.
Days and nights and weeks went by
but Jody never moved at all.

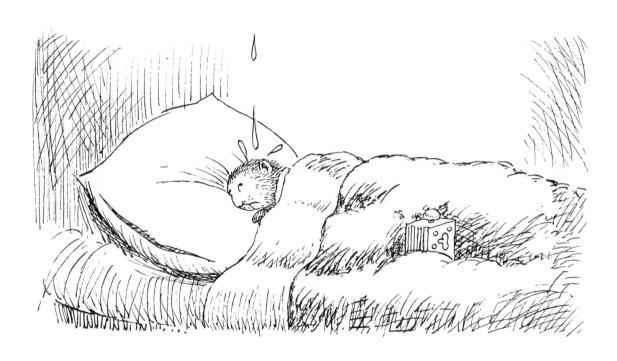

Drip. Drip.
Jody's nose twitched.
Drip. Drip. Twitch. Twitch.
Tick. Tick. Tick.
Jody opened one eye. SPLAT!
She blinked and opened the other.

On all sides water was dripping into the burrow.
Jody grumbled and pulled the covers over her head.

Suddenly she sat up straight and whistled.
"That's the snow melting—it must be spring!"
Jody jumped out of bed
and ran to the top of the burrow.
There wasn't a sound in the world.
The sun was shining. There was a soft breeze.
Suddenly she saw a white flower.
"The first flower," she whispered.
"The first flower of spring."

Jody ran through the fields shouting,
"It's Spring! It's Spring!"
Slowly, the squirrels and the snails,
the rabbits and raccoons,
the turtles and the bears
came out of their holes.
"I did it!" cried Jody. "You're all up!
"Come look at the flower.
Feel the sun. Run in the breeze.
It's going to be a wonderful spring."

The rabbit rubbed his nose and smiled at her.
"It's nice having a groundhog," he said.
"We haven't been up so early in years."